For Berit

Copyright © 2012 by Jeanette Winter

All rights reserved. Published in the United States by Schwartz & Wade Books,

an imprint of Random House Children's Books, a division of Random House, Inc., New York.

Schwartz & Wade Books and the colophon are trademarks of Random House, Inc.

Visit us on the Web! www.randomhouse.com/kids

Educators and librarians, for a variety of teaching tools, visit us at www.randomhouse.com/teachers

Library of Congress Cataloging-in-Publication Data

Winter, Jeanette.

Kali's song / Jeanette Winter.—1st ed.   p. cm.

Summary: Thousands and thousands of years ago, a young boy gets his first hunting bow

and learns to shoot, but he prefers to use the bow to make music.

ISBN 978-0-375-87022-4 (trade) — ISBN 978-0-375-97022-1 (glb)

[1. Prehistoric peoples—Fiction. 2. Cave dwellers—Fiction. 3. Music—Fiction. 4. Hunting—Fiction.] I. Title.

PZ7.W7547Kal 2012   [E]—dc22

2011009357

The text of this book is set in Equipoize Sans.

The illustrations were rendered in acrylic paint, pen and ink, and handmade paper.

MANUFACTURED IN CHINA

10 9 8 7 6 5 4 3 2 1

First Edition

Kali's Song

jeanette winter

schwartz & wade books · new york

Thousands
and
thousands
and thousands
of years ago

a boy watched his mother paint animals on a cave wall.

To the boy, the painted animals were beautiful—

just like the animals he saw on the plains.

"Kali, soon you'll be a man," his mother said.

"Soon you'll hunt and kill animals like these."

His father gave the boy a bow.

"Practice, Kali, for your first hunt," he said.

Kali practiced shooting arrows all day.

When he finally sat down to rest,

he idly plucked the string on his bow.

Kali liked the sound.

He plucked the string again.

Then, still plucking, he put the bow to his lips.

As he opened and closed his mouth,

new sounds filled the quiet air.

Kali forgot about shooting arrows
and plucked his bowstring into the night.
The stars came close to listen.

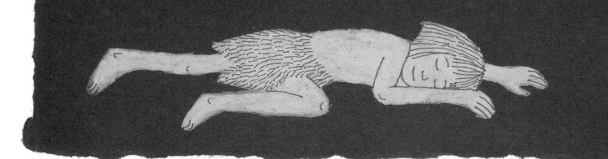

That night, the sounds from Kali's bow
filled his dreams with peace.

Every day Kali went far off to practice shooting arrows.

And every day, when he was out of sight of the caves,

he laid the arrows down,

put the bow to his mouth,

and plucked the string.

Animals listened

and were still.

Birds listened

and were still.

And the stars came close to listen.

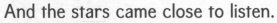

When his father asked how practice had gone,
Kali closed his eyes and said, "Good."

On the day of the big hunt,
Kali watched the sun rise.
The string on his bow was taut
and his arrows sharp.

The men led the way.
Excited boys followed,
over hills and valleys and across vast plains.

Finally, the leader spotted animals in the distance—
mammoths that were bigger and more beautiful
than any Kali had ever seen.

Kali ran to a hilltop for a closer look.

When he saw the magnificent herd below him,

he forgot about the hunt,

and he forgot about the other hunters.

He just heard the music of his bowstring in his head.

Kali laid his arrows on the grass,

put the bow to his mouth,

closed his eyes,

and played,

and played,

and played.

When Kali opened his eyes,
the mammoths were close enough to touch.
They heard the sounds from his bow,
and came to listen.

The hunters followed the herd
to the hill where Kali played.
All was quiet.
The only sound was the thrum of the bow.

The hunters laid down their arrows and bows
and listened.

"Kali uses his weapon to charm the mammoths,
not kill them."
"Only a shaman can do this."
"Kali must be a shaman."

When word of Kali's magic reached his mother,
she mixed new colors from the earth
and painted the story of Kali's song.
It made Kali proud.

As Kali grew into a man,
the tribe looked to him for guidance.

Kali cured the sick

and talked to the ancestor spirits.

And every evening,
even when he was a very old man,
Kali went to the hills with his bow,
closed his eyes, and played his bow-harp
until the stars came close to listen.